LIFE BEFORE DAMAGED
VOLUME 9

THE FERRO FAMILY

BY:

H.M. WARD

LAREE BAILEY PRESS

www.SexyAwesomeBooks.com

COPYRIGHT

This book is a work of fiction. Names, characters, places, and incidents are either the product of the author's imagination or are used fictitiously, and any resemblance to actual persons, living or dead, events, or locales is entirely coincidental.

LAREE BAILEY PRESS
First Edition: September 2015
ISBN: 9781630350895

LIFE BEFORE DAMAGED

Volume 9

LOVE KILLS PASSION

November 16th, 10:17am

I'm in love with Peter Ferro.

Damn it! How the hell did I let this happen? I hug my knees to my chest and hold on tightly, trying to squeeze the feeling from my body. It doesn't work. How could my heart betray me like this? I can't be in love with one of the manwhore brothers. It's true, Pete has moments where he shines, where he's tender, passionate, and caring. I've fallen in love with that version of Peter. I want to cling to those moments, but they're like an exploding star. Those moments are fleeting, and I'm stuck competing with the other women who are eternally in his orbit.

Footsteps draw nearer. I press my ear to the door, simultaneously afraid he's found me and hopeful he finally came looking for me.

"Gina, dammit! Where are you? We need to talk, and I'm not yelling something like this from the hallway." That voice brings forth emotions within me that I can't identify. He's not angry, not quite arrogant. I've never heard him like this. Every instinct I have urges me to rush to him, but I can't. I can't move. I'm crippled, leaning against the thick wooden door. I wonder how many women have cried against it, pouring their hearts out, knowing no one would ever hear their distress or truly care.

His voice is calmer this time, more like he's chanting to himself as he pads past my door. "Damn it."

He stops, just outside the door. I place a hand on the hard wooden surface. For a moment, I pretend I'm touching Pete the way I was in the ballroom. I move my hand quickly from the door, rubbing my palms against my thighs vigorously, wanting to wipe away any trace of him. He was with another woman. My little squabble with Anthony disrupted his moment of bliss with Miss Perfect. I wish I could disappear.

Pete's footfalls echo down the hall, becoming fainter with each step and silence settles over me. I start to shiver. I back away from the door until I bump into something hard behind me. My heart stops for a beat.

In my attempt to evade Pete, I didn't take note of which halls I ran down. I could be anywhere. I spin on the balls on my feet and take in my surroundings. Relief followed by another pang of heartache hits me in consecutive waves. I haven't strayed into forbidden territory, but what I see here is painful. There's a massive mahogany desk, a soft leather couch, and stacks of musty old books strewn across every surface.

I'm in Pete's study.

My fingers caress the smooth wood, remembering our first encounter. I rest my palms on the desk and let out a silent sob. This room is where it all began, where he offered to--in his words--fuck me thoroughly and hard. I walk around the desk, looking at the books he's reading. A battered copy of Yeats' poetry has a single bookmark peeking out from its yellowed pages. I open the book and tears sting my eyes. It's the poem he recited to me that first night, *When You Are Old.*

The memory of him speaking echoes through the empty room:

Sex isn't love. In fact, your storybook notion of love is killing your passion until one day all you'll feel for each other is numbness and resentment. It leaves you with a husband who satisfies his hunger for lust outside of your sacred love.

Oh, God! I can't do this. This can't be my life. I can't stand by like this while he falls for his mistresses. I can’t be the woman begging for leftover scraps of his emotions. I have to find a way to push him out of my heart. There's a good, caring man waiting for me tonight. I need to see him. If Pete can fall in love with a mistress, maybe I can learn to love Philip.

Screw it. No regrets. I need to get out of here, now. The chauffeurs may not be permitted to drive me anywhere, but Constance never mentioned anything about my leaving the grounds on my own.

With a determined stride, I make my way across the room and open the door a crack. When the coast is clear, I head for the garages.

STEALING... UH, BORROWING A CAR

November 16th, 10:34am

Awh. Crap!

I stare blankly at the wall-mounted box in front of me. Keys! There's a set for every car in the collection, and since it's a sizeable collection there are a million keys. Each set hangs from a little hook, above which hangs a golden plaque engraved with the make and model of a car. This should be easy, but it's not. How the hell am I supposed to tell one from another? It's not like it's the Kia lineup of six cars. Those are easily identifiable because they don't make twenty versions of sedans.

But this? The Ferros must love their cars, because I appear to be standing in the Bugatti section of an indoor car lot. Sports cars, all black, all sick-looking, all incredibly similar. Same problem with the Ferraris, the Aston Martins, and the Paganis.

Frick. I don't have time to pick a key and try it in every lock until it works. Scanning the box, I spot a set with one of those remote thingies that unlock doors from a distance. The little plaque above reads: Porsche. I grab the remote and click the unlock symbol. Lights blink on a sleek charcoal grey car, and I run toward it. I can't believe I'm stealing a car. This is so wrong, and so dangerous, and so freaking awesome! Adrenaline pumps through my veins, bringing me back to life. I've missed the rush.

I yank open the door and slide onto the buttery leather seat. I glance down at the gear shifter, relieved. It's an automatic. I never learned to drive a stick. Dad always insisted a princess deserved to be chauffeured around. God, that sounds pretentious. I look around the steering wheel but can't find the slot to insert the key. My eyes scan the dashboard. Nothing.

"Uh, car? Start engine? Vroomy-vroomy?" I feel like an idiot talking to a car--especially when nothing happens. There goes that idea. A voice-operated car would have been cool.

I study the key-remote-thingy closer. FML! There's no actual key to it. It looks more like a small vibrator than a key. I prod and poke everywhere, trying to figure out how to get this damn car started. Keys! It's not an entirely outdated concept, people!

I rest my forehead on the steering wheel. That's when I see it. There's a little slot to the left of the steering wheel, right on the dashboard. I try to fit the whole remote in the slot. It works! The engine purrs smoothly to life, and I suddenly get why guys are so into cars. The sound is erotic.

I shift into drive, press my foot down gently on the gas pedal, and the car takes off like a bullet. My head slams back into the headrest. I stomp both feet on the brake and lock my hands in a death grip on the steering wheel. The car comes to an abrupt stop, tires squealing, barely missing the little red convertible in front of me.

"Ho-ly, that was close!"

With trembling hands and wobbly, barely-responsive legs, I back up slowly, readjust the car's path and maneuver it past the archway into the garages, and outside. I expect him to hear me and come running after the car, but there's no sign of Pete. He probably went back to boinking the chick in the sheets. Tears sting my eyes and I take a shaky breath as I race down the Long Island Expressway. I don't care how fast I'm going or if I get pulled over. Screw Constance. Before I know it, I'm at Erin's apartment.

After jumping out of the car, I take the stairs two at a time and pound my fist on Erin's door. I hear the familiar sounds of chains and locks from the other side, metal sliding against metal. She opens the door and grins before attacking me with a ginormous hug that would put bears to shame. The word inappropriate comes to mind. She's wearing a towel around her waist. Thank God she's wearing something on top. I pry her freakishly strong arms from around me. She takes a step back and looks me up and down, unable to believe I'm here. I barely believe it myself.

"Holy eff, Gina! What are you doing here?"

"I needed to escape. Mind if I hang here?"

Erin places both hands on either side of my face and studies me. I need her to be crass right now. I don't want to think about why I'm really here. "I don't mind at all," she says biting her lip, and then looks over her shoulder. "I was kind of in the middle of something buuuut..."

Her friendly smile morphs into an expression I know all too well. It's THE LOOK, the one that has gotten us into trouble so many times as kids, the one I've been hoping to see. "Why don't you join me? I'm gonna make you try something completely out of your comfort zone, princess."

"Uh..."

WTF DID I JUST DO?

November 16th, 7:46pm

"So thanks for stopping by, and we'll call you again soon. Talented hands like that are hard to find." Erin gives Whatever-His-Name-Is some money, then closes the door behind him. She walks back over to where I'm standing, placing herself behind me and pushing my hair over to one side, clearing my left shoulder.

"I can't believe we did this, Gee. I've been waiting for so long, I just never thought I'd do it with you. Wasn't it amazing? You know, I'm kinda proud of you. Virgins are usually more discreet their first time. This is just--wow! I mean, look at you! You look so beautiful," Erin gushes. She's forcing me to see my reflection in her mirror. WTF did I do?

I turn around halfway and swat Erin on the arm. "Shut up. We'll call it extreme cherry popping and leave it at that. I'm never doing this again. Holy shiznit!" I speak Yiddish now. All the kids are doing it. I turn my back to her and look at myself in the mirror with disbelief.

"Of course you're doing this again. It's addictive. Especially considering how bitchin' you look. Hot damn, baby-cakes!" Erin says proudly, using her foot to kick away her sweat pants and my top from around our feet on the floor.

I let out a nervous laugh, "Baby-cakes? You need to stop hanging around Ricky."

Erin's face drops when I mention Ricky. There's something there she's not telling me. Our eyes meet in the mirror, and she puts on a plastic smile. I open my mouth to ask, but she cuts me off. "Hold still. This may sting like a bitch, but it's part of the fun!"

I nod and stare at myself in the mirror. No more regrets, Gina. The thrill of what I've just done is slowly catching up. I don't care how much trouble I'm going to get into over this. This is for me. This is me, now more than ever.

Standing in nothing but my bra and jeans, I turn around to take a look at my back in the mirror, and it's just as amazing as the front. Big red roses, linked together by thorn-covered stems, decorate my left shoulder. They spill onto the upper part of my arm and cascade down onto my shoulder blade. Underneath the roses, a black lace-like pattern adds femininity and delicateness to the design. It's perfect.

I needed a clear reminder of who I was, who I am, and who I want to be. With everything that's happened, I don't want to lose myself in the chaos. Pete's right--I am like a rose, both delicate and strong all at once. Handle me roughly and my petals may wilt, but not before you feel the sting of my thorns.

I wince when Erin touches me. Applying the ointment stings like a wicked sunburn and I inhale sharply, biting down on my bottom lip to keep from yelping out in pain.

"So you don't think Mama Ferro is going to murder you for this?" Erin's tone is mischievous. "What about that good girl image clause? Wasn't that to make them look more amiable in the public eye?" With the ointment, my tattoo glistens under the loft's overhead lighting.

"Screw my image." My chest squeezes painfully around my lungs. My eyes burn with the all too familiar feeling of tears begging to escape.

I'm so sick of crying over Peter Ferro. I don't want to love him, but I do. Meanwhile, he loves someone else--whatever his newfound notion of love is.

I bend down to pick up my top, but can't put it back on. It has sleeves. "Erin? Can I borrow one of your halter-tops? This thing's gonna hurt." I glance at my friend in the mirror. She gives me a skeptical look before nodding and running up to her room to retrieve a sexy, bust-enhancing, halter-top.

I put it on and study my reflection. I'm going to look so hot for Philip! The thought rips me up inside. He should be the one I'm in love with, not Pete. Philip cares for me.

Erin steps in between the mirror and me. "Gina? What's that look? Why are you here, anyway? I know you're not allowed to come here, yet here you are. Obviously, something's wrong, I can feel it, and don't just make something up. Spill girl. What happened?"

I look off to the side, unable to meet her gaze. "Nothing's changed." Everything's changed. "Pete & I will still get engaged when that ball drops on New Year's Eve." The thought should have me squeeing like a schoolgirl at a boy-band concert, but it doesn't.

"So, what happened?"

I tell Erin and my voice breaks as I speak, coming out in a sobby slew of sounds. I'm incoherent, but that's okay. She understands me like no one else.

Erin asks, "She's not just anybody, is she?" I shake my head, unable to answer. "Oh, Gina. I'm so sorry. Listen, I have an important meeting with the owner of an art gallery in an hour, and I really can't miss it. His schedule is weird, and this was the only time he could fit me in. But spend the night here and when I get back, we'll eat popcorn and pizza and watch TV." Erin gives me a look of pity, and I hate it. I need to be stronger. I take a deep breath and smile. This could be a big day for her.

"You go to your meeting and kick ass. I think I may hang out at the club tonight. Philip invited me, and I'm dying to get out and socialize with normal people again."

Erin's eyebrows scrunch with disapproval. "Really? Philip was pissed after you dumped his ass for the sexperienced sexpert."

"I know but he apologized for his reaction, and I think he may want us to get back together. Why should I turn my back on someone who really cares about me? Especially when I like him too?"

Erin pushes my hair aside, over to my right shoulder and studies my tattoo before looking up into my eyes. "Tell you what. If you need a fuck buddy to help you get over Ferro, we'll go man hunting tomorrow night. I may know of a few available pork swords that would love to take you for a ride down the steamin' semen roadway. Just not Philip's, okay? I don't want you to get hurt."

"I appreciate the concern, Erin, but you don't need to worry about me. Philip can't break my heart, we're not like that."

"Oh, princess, it's not your heart I'm worried about."

BREAKING NEWS, EVERYBODY!

November 16th, 9:15pm

I feel horrible about lying to Erin. I told her I'd wait for her to finish her meeting and then we'd spend a quiet evening together. I knew it was a lie as I said it.

Sitting in the hot Porsche, I lower the visor and look at my reflection. I've changed so much in the past couple of months. So far the changes have been for the better, but I'm not so sure about the alterations that will take place after this. Tonight isn't just a cosmetic change. Tonight I'll take values I've always considered important and toss them in the trash. I'm about to be miserably married with a lover on the side. "Well, it's now or never, Jenny. Let's find out what you're made of."

I put the finishing touches on my black, cat-eye eyeliner and cherry red lipstick. I flip the visor back up and open the car door, stepping out into the cold night air and making my way toward Ricky's club.

"Gina."

I freeze when I hear my name fall from those lips. Pete. My head tells me to keep walking, but everything else pulls me toward him.

"Gina?" It comes out as a question, almost as if he's no longer sure I'm me. I close my eyes briefly, take a deep breath, and turn slowly.

"This is getting old, Pete. How did you find me this time? Did you chip me like a pet, or am I that predictable?"

Pete laughs once, but it's a hollow, empty laugh, almost as tired as his voice. "You are the farthest thing from predictable." His hands reflexively rub his face, remembering the slap I gave him. His eyes cut to my shoulder, taking in my new ink as he takes a tentative step toward me. "Your list of go-to spots is short, and it helps that you left your cellphone on your bed, open to a message telling Gambino you're meeting him here tonight."

I try to remain calm, even though I'm fuming inside. I say placidly, "You went in my room? You looked through my things? Did you have a good time?" I feel my bitch face sharpen the words as I ice over.

"Considering the circumstances, I had every right to try and find you. Besides," Pete lifts a single eyebrow and looks over to the Porsche, "That was a gutsy move, Granz, stealing my mother's favorite car. If you're lucky, we'll get it home before she notices it's gone. She's likely to kill someone if she thinks her precious baby is missing." Pete looks impressed, but the expression disappears quickly, replaced by the serious, no-nonsense version of Pete. It doesn't jive with his leather jacket tousled hair, and stubbled jaw. "Come on, Gina. Let's get out of here. You and I need to talk."

Pete takes my hand and pulls me toward his bike. It's parked in the shadows at the far end of the parking lot. No wonder I didn't see him when I pulled in.

"No." It's one word that changes everything. I don't want to be dragged off. I don't want to hear his explanations.

The cold winter wind cuts into my skin like little knives. My halter-top does nothing to keep me warm, and I'm regretting leaving my sweater at Erin's. It was only supposed to be a few steps from the car to the bar.

Pete's fingers uncurl from mine, and he releases me. I wrap my arms around myself to ward off the cold, and rub my arms vigorously with my hands, careful not to touch the tattoo.

Pete takes off his leather jacket and hands it to me. "Here. You're riding with me on the bike. I'll send someone for the car." He's wearing a dark, tight-fitting turtleneck sweater that hugs every toned muscle of his chest. He looks warm and comfy, and it makes me think of cuddles in front of a warm fire with mugs of hot chocolate and marshmallows.

I glance at his jacket longingly, really wanting to take it and wrap myself in its warmth, but I don't. I stand defiantly, shaking my head, teeth chattering and rubbing my arms.

This action earns me the Pete Ferro blazing blue eyes of fury—sending tingles up my spine. "Gina, put the coat on now and get on the bike." He shoves the jacket my way again, but I stand my ground, still rubbing my arms. It's cold enough that each exhaled breath forms a puffy white cloud in the air between us. My legs tremble, shivering with cold, but I won't give in.

I plaster my most charming smile to my lips, and reply sweetly--the way my mother acts in public. I know it'll piss him off, and I look forward to his rebuttal like some sick form of foreplay. "What exactly did you want to tell me, darling? It's getting a little nippy, and I really must go indoors before I catch a chill. Nothing? Well, thank you for checking up on me, then. It was very courteous of you. Please tell your mother I'll be back before dawn and will return the car promptly. Have a good evening, sir."

Mental translation: tell your Mom she can suck a lemon and then fuck herself with it because I won't come running every time she calls. I turn on my heels and start to walk toward the bar.

"Dammit, Gina! Get on this bike and come home with me." Pete's voice is a low rumble, dangerous and sexy.

I've been trying to keep it together, but hearing him speak that way is like blasphemy. My heart aches at the sound of it, and I long for things I can no longer have. These people keep finding ways to hurt me over and over again.

I turn around to face him once more, my hair whipping around and hitting me in the face. "Home?" I laugh but there's no joy to it. I press my fingers to my chest and bite out the words. "I don't have a home. Not anymore. You and your family made sure of that. This place, right here," I jab my thumb over my shoulder, toward the club, "has been more of a home to me than anywhere else in the past couple of months. You may have given me a roof over my head, but home is where a person feels both safe and loved. At your house, there is neither."

Pete's expression falters, losing a bit of its edgy bite. He works his jaw, and I can tell he wants to say something, but he's holding himself back, shaking his head until he mutters, "If you only knew."

I laugh once, loudly. This is a sick joke. There's nothing to know. I step toward him and get up in his face. "If I only knew what, Pete? Huh? If I only knew how you all think that everyone outside of your precious family is worthless, including me? Is that it? Yes! You've made it very clear and flaunting all those women in front of me makes me feel very loved. Thank you so much. What else is there? Oh, yes! I almost forgot the fact that your mother is constantly watching every single step I make, following me around, trying to catch me doing something wrong so she can toss my ass in jail. Again, I'm very much aware, and it makes me feel very safe. Oh, and by the way," my hands drop to my sides and ball into fists as I rise up on my toes and scream, "I'M BEING SARCASTIC!"

Pete just watches me from an inch away, not speaking. Those eyes are filled with pain and remorse, but I'm not falling for it—not again. It doesn't matter what I see in him, because it's not really there. The man is a walking illusion. He uses whatever he can to get anything he wants. For a while he wanted me—to toy with, to fuck, to add to his long list of conquests.

He inches closer and it makes my heart jerk inside my chest. I know I'm the one who got this close to him, but now I want to back away. I dig my heels in. This fight determines our future. "I'm not spending the rest of my life in a living mausoleum. Screw that. I've sacrificed my happiness to protect your family, yet that doesn't seem to be enough—"

"Gina." He says my name like a plea, but I don't stop.

"They always want more. There's always another fee to pay, another role to perform. It's sucked me dry. This is the only thing I have left that brings me any joy. You're not going to take it away."

Suddenly, we're standing toe-to-toe, and he points his finger toward the club. I have to tilt my head to keep eye contact with him. His eyes are a mix of anger and pain, and the more I spew my feelings at him, the more he looks like I'm cutting him to shreds, flaying him raw.

Pete talks, but his jaw doesn't move. It's clenched too tight. The muscles bulge in his cheeks. "You have everything so wrong. Those people in there aren't safe, and they don't love you. I don't want you anywhere near them. I don't trust them."

I toss my arms up in the air. "Oh, what a surprise! Breaking news, everybody! A Ferro that doesn't trust someone. Well, that's certainly a first! I have news for you, Pete. It's in your DNA to not trust anyone. You are so convinced everyone has an ulterior motive that you can't see the good in anyone anymore. They aren't bad people, Pete. They're my friends, and they look out for me."

Pete takes a step back and runs a hand through his hair in exasperation, coat still dangling from his other hand. He paces around in a small circle before he rounds on me again. He leans down so that our faces are only inches apart. His voice is a hiss through his clenched teeth, his jaw muscles twitching. We aren't touching, but I am aware of every inch of him. The moment feels charged, the air crackling between us like a high voltage current.

Pete explodes, "For once in your life, listen to me and WAKE UP! Those people in there are lying to you! They want you for your connection to me. They don't care about you. There are a lot of things I will tolerate, Gina. I can stand by watching as you pull extreme stunts like skydiving or stealing my mom's car. I can even feed your need for danger myself, taking turns so sharp on my bike that I worry we won't make it back alive. I do it because of your laugh, the way your face lights up, the sparkle in your eyes--they're all breathtaking. It's infectious, and I need more of it, I crave it."

I want to put my hands over my ears. They're suddenly pressing the sides of my head. "Stop! I don't want to hear this!"

He grabs hold of my wrists and yanks them away. "No! Listen to me, Gina. You matter to me. It makes me want to be alive just to experience it over and over again. Then you turn around and get your body tattooed, and it makes you look so damned beautiful that all I can think about right now is running my hands over every inch of your body." Pete's eyes look down while his hand hovers over my shoulder. He releases my wrists, but I can still feel the searing heat shooting through my skin as if he was still touching me.

His hand clenches into a trembling fist, and he shuts his eyes tight. "But even I have my limits. There is no way in hell I will stand by quietly and watch these people take advantage of the only woman I've ever loved in my whole sorry excuse for a life!"

AFTERSHOCK

November 16th, 9:23pm

Silence.

Pete and I stand motionless, breathing hard. I feel neither hot nor cold. My teeth are chattering, my entire body shivering, but I'm not sure if it's from the weather or from what he just said. I feel like I've just been through the spin cycle of a washing machine.

Pete looks like he's in shock. It's as if he's said something he never intended to admit. His face has gone white, his eyes open wide as plates, and he covers his mouth with his hand like he's trying to take back what he said.

This can't be real.

Pete is the first to move. He runs a hand through his hair and reaches out to touch me. I can't let him. I stumble backward a step. Ok, maybe it's more like tripping over my shoes and ungracefully losing my balance, arms flailing. I screech. I'm about to land on my ass, but Pete is quick and catches me by the waist, pulling me close to him. His warmth and his touch are welcoming, but after what he just said I can't do this. My brain will short-circuit again, and I'll start believing him.

His arms circle my waist and hold me tightly, keeping my cheek pressed to his chest. His heart is beating fast and hard, like he's running for his life. He rests his head on top of mine. I keep my hands fisted, arms tucked between us, ready to push him away. I'm being soothed by the rhythm of his rapid breathing.

My body goes stiff as I try to fight off the impulse to melt into his arms.

This isn't happening.

It's not real.

It can't be.

Peter Ferro did not just confess that he loves me. But he did. I heard it. I can't fathom why he'd say it. It can't be true. This isn't like him.

Pete's hands travel up my back, one laces through my hair, cradling my head, keeping me close to his chest. He drops a small kiss on the top of my head and holds me tighter. His whole body is trembling.

"Let me go," I say weakly, trying to break free.

Distance. I need distance.

He loosens his hold on me, but he doesn't let me get away from him. He stares down at me, pain etched across his face. When he swallows, I see his Adam's apple bob up and down like he's just swallowed a football. "I can't let you go, Gina. I know I should, and I tried, but I can't."

Pete exhales and leans in, pressing his forehead against mine before closing his eyes. He looks like he's attempting to shut out the world around him, and my traitor heart breaks for him, wanting to comfort him. His warm breath spills across my face, and it's dizzying. I stare at his mouth so close to mine. How I'd love to close the space between us, to feel the softness of his lips on mine once more, but I can't.

Pete's voice cracks when he talks. He's fighting off words that are coming out without his consent. "I've tried so hard to fight this, to let you go, to push you away. But I can't, Gina. I can't. How can someone so small and sweet manage to cause so much damage? But you did. You crashed into my life like a train coming in at full speed--I had no chance of surviving the impact. You've broken me. I never wanted to feel anything for anyone, but you made me decimate the one rule I swore I'd never break."

"Asking a chick over to your mansion bachelor pad isn't a super-hard rule to break."

Pete exhales shakily. "Not that rule. I promised myself I'd never make the mistake of falling in love. What have you done to me?"

When Pete opens his eyes again, there is no anger left. There's just desperation and immense fear. Pete Ferro is never scared. He's reckless, angry, and passionate, but I've never seen him scared of anything--until now. With another trembling breath he exhales, "Gina, I love you."

I want to hold him tight, to kiss him hard and soft, to ease his fears, to tell him I love him, too, but I can't tell him how I feel. What if he's lying, again? Like that kiss in Central Park. It seemed so real in the moment, and I believed him. He'll just hurt me more if it's not true. It can't be this simple, can it? I've cared for Pete too many times, and he crushed my heart each and every one. I'm never good enough for him. He has no clue what love means. He has another woman waiting for him at the mansion. I saw her.

I struggle to free myself from him and this time he lets me. Without his arms around me, without the intense warmth of his body, I start to shiver again. Pete stares down at the ground, defeated and lost. He looks like a little boy lost in a crowd. His hands are twisting the supple jacket. When he talks, his voice has no spirit left in it. "I've tried to do the right thing from the start. My methods may not have been best, but I promise I'll fix things for you. I was hoping that we could have this conversation back at the house, but I guess it's too late for that."

I don't understand. Shaking my head, I glance down at the sidewalk and back up at him. "What are you talking about?"

"I'm turning myself in." He chances a glance up to me, under his lashes. "I'm going to the police tomorrow and confessing. I'm going to tell them that everything was my fault--the trespassing, the rave, the assault, the manslaughter, the arson, everything. I'm going to jail for this and I've accepted it. It's the only way to give you back your life, because you don't deserve this." He offers a painful smile.

He lowers his gaze and then looks back into my eyes. "I guess this is goodbye." Pete takes one of my hands in his and turns it over, before he presses a soft kiss to the center of my palm. He folds my fingers over the kiss, trapping it in my fist. Then he lets go, turns around, and walks over to his bike.

DON'T LEAVE ME

November 16th, 9:31pm

I stand there shaking, lost between a world that I thought was vacant and meaningless. But as it comes apart around me, I feel like I'm being torn in half. He can't do this. He can't go to jail and take the blame for me. If it weren't for me, there wouldn't have been a rave.

I'm torn between wanting to hate him and panicking at the thought of not seeing him anymore. I'm caught in an emotional freefall as my convictions tell me I can't let him take the blame for something I did. My morals swirl rapidly in my mind, forming a twister of thoughts and reasons why he can't do this. But the main words repeating in the rush are these:

Don't leave me.

He's almost reached his bike. If he gets to it, he'll ride off, and I'll never see him again. I run. My feet slap hard against the pavement as I rush at him. "Stop! Wait!"

By the time I get to the bike, he's already straddled it and has the key in the ignition. He looks up at me.

I speak without thinking. "Wh-why would you do something like that? I need you, Pete. Don't do this! We made a deal. You can't break it. What'll happen to me?" My mind is going over the implications. If he goes through with this, if he breaks the deal we made—I don't know what his mother will do.

Pete stops and gives me a small smile. It's not genuine. It doesn't reach his eyes like it does when we're dancing. "You'll be fine, Gina. I told you I was going to fix things for you. Can you believe I actually managed to outwit my mother? I convinced her to transfer ownership of the company to me now instead of waiting for our wedding day. Granz Textiles is mine. All along, she only wanted the patent, so I sold it to Ferro Corp. By tomorrow, the company will be back in your father's hands. As for your criminal file, I destroyed it. There is no way to prove you're linked to the rave anymore. Besides, once they have my confession, they won't need to arrest anyone else. Sending a Ferro to jail will be more than enough to appease the masses. Lord knows there's enough venom toward our family after Sean's trial. I couldn't care less about going to jail, and my family's reputation is the least of my worries. The Ferro name is tarnished no matter what I do."

His logic makes no fucking sense. "Then why did you ever agree to our engagement in the first place? Why are you doing this now?"

"Can't you see? It's always been about you, Gina. Right from the start, every dumbass thing I've said, every cruel thing I've done, it was all to protect you." He sits on his bike and holds out the helmet and jacket. "Come with me. Let me hold you one last time."

I want to. I want to so much, but the questions run wild in my head, clouding my thoughts. "Since when?" I'm afraid to ask the full question, scared the reporters will jump out and have their story and this farce will end. I swallow hard, unable to look him in the eye.

"You want to know when I realized I was falling in love with you?" I nod. Pete's eyebrows come together in the middle, creating a cute little crinkle that I want to smooth out with my fingers. Understanding comes over his face and when he replies there is no bluster left in his voice--only sadness. It's the look that comes with remembering something bittersweet. "You started something in me on the first day we met, but it was really the morning when I woke up with you in my bed, in my arms. The morning we went riding on my bike for the first time. That's when I knew."

That was the morning after the Jenny fiasco. The day after Anthony cheated on me. But that can't be right. He had me in his bed, practically naked, and he still pushed me away. I shake my head so slightly it's barely noticeable.

His eyes are pleading, like believing him is the most important thing ever. I want to believe him, but the risks are too high. I stare at the jacket and helmet, desperately wanting to get on that bike, to hold on tight and never let go. I want so badly to have my Happily Ever After with someone who will love me with all his heart, someone who will put me first and see only me. Can I trust Pete to be that person? I start to lift my trembling hands, ready to take the leap of faith, but a little voice inside stops me.

He's not in love with you. Ferros are incapable of love.

The spell breaks and I drop my hands. I can't.

He sees me as that silly girl who still believes Prince Charming will sweep me off my feet and ride off into the sunset. The time for fairytales is over.

"Why tell me now? If it's been that long, why didn't you say anything sooner? Why the games? Why did you keep on pushing me away?"

"Come back with me, and I'll tell you everything. Please come home with me, Gina. Don't go in there." Pete is pleading with me, his voice stern, but obviously worried.

I turn to look back at the club, where warmth and friendship are waiting for me. I can't see what he's telling me. I don't see how they're bad, using me, or anything else. It's a place to dance and laugh. It's a place that makes me happy filled with people who care about me.

I push the jacket and the helmet away from me, shaking my head. "I can't trust my feelings when I'm around you. I need space and some time to think. I'm sorry, Peter. I'll be back later tonight, and I promise we'll talk. Will you wait up for me?" I place a hand on his cheek, and he leans in just a tiny bit and closes his eyes.

"Of course I will. Go in there and have fun, but be careful."

"I will."

I take a step back and break the contact between us. Pete puts on his jacket and helmet. After lowering his visor, he revs up the engine and takes off. I stand in the cold parking lot, watching his taillight disappear into the night until I can no longer hear the roar of his bike.

MR. RIGHT

November 16th, 9:57pm

Walking back to the club takes forever. It feels like I fell down a wormhole and got spit out in Jersey. Pete's words swirl together in my head until I feel like it may explode. I tug on the door, but it won't open. It's locked. There are cars in the parking lot, so the club should be open. I knock a couple of times, peeking in through the window. I bounce up and down on the balls of my feet and rub my arms some more, in between knocks. Philip's handsome face peers through the glass door. He smiles warmly at me before unlocking and opening the door.

I step inside into a rush of heat, but I don't feel any warmer. My skin is still pebbled with goose bumps and no matter how much I rub my arms, the heat won't reach my bones. It feels like I'm in shock. Philip takes me into a brief, friendly hug, but that's all I get. No tingles, no giddiness. Maybe I'm still just too numb after everything that just happened with Peter.

Philip cups my face with his hands and searches my eyes. I want to look away, but I can't. Guilt at how we parted the last time forces me to make eye-contact with him. I just hope I'm not misleading him again. I'm not going back to his place tonight after all.

"I'm so glad you were able to make it, Gina. You look frozen. Did you walk all the way here from Ferro's house without a coat?"

I force a smile at Philip, shaking my head. "No, I drove." I look down at my left shoulder. "Trying not to let anything touch this. Hurts like a bitch."

Philip takes in my new ink job. "Wow! It looks amazing. Come on in and warm up. The guys are here and can't wait to see you again." Philip locks the door behind me and places a hand on my lower back, escorting me inside.

I wander into the club, still dazed and confuzzled by Pete's outburst outside. It's like walking through thick fog. You only notice things once they are in your face. There's no music. In fact, the club is empty, save Philip and his skydiving crew. They sit around a table, playing poker and smoking cigars while Ricky busily mixes drinks and loads them on a tray.

"Oh, hell yeah! The pussy has arrived." Zeke, Philip's disturbingly gross friend, seems much too enthusiastic at my arrival. I suppress a disgusted shiver when I hear his voice. He puts both hands behind his head, props his feet on the table and balances back on the two hind legs of his chair. He winks at me and makes a disgusting, suggestive flicking gesture with his pierced tongue. I hope never to be alone in a room with that guy. I'd mace him in the face.

Philip's grip on my back tightens, and he leans in close to say, "Don't mind Zeke, he's being a prick as usual tonight."

I wave toward the table, "Hey, guys! Good to see you again." I answer back lightly. I don't want Zeke to see just how much he gets to me. Most of the guys acknowledge me with brief waves and mumbles.

Zeke, however, looks at me intently, overtly checking me out from head to toe. "Oh, I'll be seeing much more of you later, babe." He points toward all of the guys sitting at the table, calling their attention to him. "I call first fuck!"

"Zeke! If you don't shut the fuck up now, you're outta here. Got it?" Philip's tone is threatening. He wraps a protective arm around my waist and pulls me in close. Funky weirdo-vibes are setting off every alarm I have and sending chills down my neck. I touch it gently and feel the hairs standing on end. Peter freaked me out with his warnings, and this is just me acting on his paranoia. Zeke scares me, but as long as Philip and Ricky are here I'm safe. I peel Philip's arm off of my back and politely excuse myself to go to the bar, where my good friend is still busy filling up the guys' orders.

"Gina? What the hell are you doing here?" Ricky whisper-yells the moment I get close to the bar. He deposits the last glass on the tray and starts to wipe down the bar with a rag.

"Philip asked me to come over. Why is this place closed tonight?"

"Because sometimes we close, Gina. It's my club, and if I decide to close it one night so my friends can hold a private meeting that's my prerogative." His reply takes me aback. I've never seen him anything but happy and welcoming. He's usually the human equivalent of a Chihuahua, always bouncing around.

"What's wrong, Ricky? Why are you so upset? I thought you'd be happy to see me, not pissed. What gives?"

Ricky shakes his head. "Never mind. Could you bring this tray over to the guys? Thanks, doll." His voice is detached, not the usual boisterous, energetic Ricky that I've come to know. Chills creep up my spine. There's something eerily wrong here.

I nod, give Ricky a weak smile and take the tray. I walk around the table, each one of the guys retrieving their drink as I pass. As I walk past Philip, he gives my backside a little pat. It's supposed to feel fun and flirty, especially considering this is why I agreed to see him in the first place. I wanted to push Pete out of my heart by replacing him with Philip, but this only feels dirty--especially after Zeke's earlier comments and Pete's warning. I don't say anything and just keep smiling.

After I finish serving the drinks, Philip pats his lap, inviting me to sit. There isn't any room for an extra chair at the table. I hesitate. I can't shake the feeling that something isn't right, and suddenly regret having come in at all.

I'm acting crazy. This is Philip Gambino. He's my fun, cute, thrill-seeking, sweet, caring man. He's my Mr. Right. Damn the Ferros and their trust issues. I shake off the feeling and sit crosswise on Philip's lap. His hand rests midway up my jean-clad thigh.

I sit in silence, watching the guys play poker, drinking, smoking their cigars and passing newspapers around. My mind starts to wander.

Pete loves me. After everything we've been through, how can I believe him? Most importantly, how can I forgive him for all the times he's hurt me. Will he be able to stop sleeping around if we're together or will the other women always be there, a distraction to spice up his boring love life? He already tried to convince me that love kills lust and Anthony shared what a horrible lover I am.

Still, he's sacrificing himself--his freedom, his fortune, his entire family's reputation—to protect me. Is it out of love or to ease his conscience? Part of the blame is mine, but he destroyed that evidence. Pete is guilty of many things, but so am I. He's giving me back my freedom, my life, my family's name and company, while he condemns himself to a lifetime in prison over what? A few shed tears and my bruised ego? That can't be right.

My mind goes in circles for a while, and no matter what thoughts occur, it comes down to one thing:

I can't let him do this.

I need to hear him out, and the only way is to go back to him, now. Tomorrow will be too late, and I'll regret it forever. If he's lying, I'm going to lose it, but if he's telling the truth, we could have a shot at being happy together.

A voice inside of me is quick to reply, but what about all those other women? The woman from earlier is still very fresh in my mind, but he never once mentioned her. There are too many questions with no answers. I'll never know if I don't give him a chance to explain his side of the story. I need to leave. Now. I have to stop Pete from turning himself in.

I start to stand up, but Philip pulls me back down on his lap, taking me by surprise. "Where do you think you're going?" He says teasingly, spreading his hand over my stomach. His touch is unwelcome, and his fingers feel like little spiders crawling all over my skin.

"I'm sorry. I know I only just got here, but I'm feeling guilty for taking one of the Ferro cars without asking. Mrs. Ferro is probably going to have my head if I don't bring it back. I really need to go. Guilty conscience and all, you know me, Sergeant Buzzkill!"

The men all burst out laughing. My joke wasn't that funny. All eyes are on me, including Philip's. The look he gives me is bizarre. "Forget about that witch," Phillip says, holding me tighter. "Stay and have a bit of fun with us."

The way he looks at me is all sorts of wrong. It's suggestive, and those little spiders of his dancing up and down my sides make me feel a bit sick to my stomach. I wriggle around a bit on his lap to get off, but he holds me close, digging his fingers into me. Now I'm starting to freak out. I don't like feeling trapped.

"No, really, Philip." I look over toward Ricky and see him watching us, an angry scowl on his face, but he doesn't move to do anything about it. I give him a quick 'help me' look, but he just turns his back and starts to dust off the bottles behind the bar.

Philip slips a hand under my shirt, working his way up toward my breasts. His other hand creeps up my thigh. I cross my legs to keep him out of unwanted territory, but that doesn't stop him from roaming upwards.

"Here's how things usually go down, Gina. During our meetings we have some paid female entertainment, but tonight, tag, you're it. So, you're going to be a good little girl, and you're going to make sure we all leave here very happy men." Philip's voice is unrecognizable. It's cold and threatening, and any trace of the gentleman I've come to know is gone.

I laugh nervously, thinking this is some sick joke. "What?"

His hand covers my breast and squeezes. My face burns bright red as embarrassment and fear drip through my stomach like acid.

"It's no big deal, Gina."

They use prostitutes. Oh my god. This can't be real. Mr. Gambino is a trustworthy politician whose spotless reputation is the key to his success. He's one of the biggest anti-corruption advocates around. How can his son be like this?

Ice water runs through my veins. I look around the table, finding all eyes on me--ravenous, greedy eyes telling me I'm the biggest fool around and I'm in a shitstorm of trouble. My heart is pounding, and my palms are sweaty. I wiggle around some more, trying to pry Philip's hands off of me, but he just presses me up against his crotch. I feel him, so hard beneath me and, this time, I feel like I may actually be sick.

"It's time someone taught the Ferros a lesson, don't you think? They cannot just take what belongs to others. You were mine, Gina, or at least you were going to be mine. We would have been the perfect couple, but Ferro just steps in and claims you for himself." He tsks his tongue in disapproval. He manages to place a hand over one of my breasts and squeezes, painfully hard. I let out a painful cry, and the guys just chuckle. I look over at Ricky once more, but he's still ignoring us, dusting his damn bottles.

"I'm surprised he chose you out of all of his sluts. There's not much to hold onto here, is there? But still, pussy is pussy." Philip looks toward Zeke. "Sorry dude, I get first fuck this time around. You'll have to wait your turn."

"RICKY!" I call out. This is his club, and he's my friend. There's no way he'll let them hurt me.

He'll help me. He'll fight them off, he'll call the cops, he'll...

"Dammit, doll! I don't like this, but we all have to make sacrifices to get by. I'm sorry. I'll leave you guys to do your thing. Don't forget to lock up before you go, and clean up your mess this time."

...he'll hand me over to a gang of rapists and turn his back on me.

TURKEY STUFFING

November 16th, 10:46pm

The door closes behind Ricky, and I'm left alone with a half-dozen men who want nothing more than to rip my clothes off and take me one after the other--or worse, all at the same time. Erin tried to warn me. Hell, so did Pete, but I didn't believe either of them. I never thought he was this messed up! Guys like Zeke should clue a girl in. The BFF is basically a reflection of Phillip. Why didn't I see it?

I need a plan. I'm small and greatly outnumbered. If I try to fight them off, it'll just encourage them to be even more forceful with me.

Philip kisses down my neck, still groping my chest in front of a pack of drooling assholes. My pulse quickens, but it's not from arousal. Fear is slowly seizing me. Every muscle in my body cords up tight, wanting to fight or freeze.

I scan the room, searching, trying to find the quickest escape route. I could run, but they'd catch up with me before I got to the car and then they'd beat the crap out of me. The restroom door doesn't lock, so that's a no-go. Ricky's office door is close enough that if I distract them, I could lock myself up in there and call the cops. Provided these guys don't know the combination on the keypad to Ricky's office, once inside, I could be safe.

Phil's wandering hands busy themselves, trying to unfasten my jeans while I struggle to remember the code to Ricky's office door. I try to pry Philip's hands off as gently as I can without it coming off as a struggle. I need a distraction. It probably won't be enough to stop him, but hopefully it'll be enough to slow him down. For this to work, I need him to lower his guard which means I need to swallow my vomit and play along.

I force a seductive smile toward Philip and lean in to whisper in his ear. "Are you sure you want to share me with your friends? You must know why I came here tonight. I'm miserable without you. I miss you. I wasn't planning on being this forward, but I want you to be my lover, Philip. Just you. I want to be yours and only yours. I told you I don't love Pete. Just think. Together, we can take down the Ferros, if that's what you want. I hate them, too, and I want to see them suffer for what they did to me, especially Pete." My voice is shaky. It doesn't sound convincing at all. I just hope that lust fogs up his perception, and he can't see my terror.

His smile quirks up. The hunger in his eyes goes from predatory to possessive. He never breaks eye contact with me when he addresses the group. "Guys, change of plans." I try not to sag in relief. It worked. "Gina's mine. Except for tonight. She needs to prove her loyalty. I get her first, and then you all get a turn," his eyes rest on each man sitting expectantly around the table, "once." His eyes meet mine again. "Deal?"

I nod and take a deep breath before leaning forward to kiss him. His kiss is nothing like I remember. Instead of being gentle and sweet, he presses his mouth forcefully against mine. The way he pushes his tongue inside my mouth feels like he's trying to stuff a turkey. His hands cling to my face, holding me locked into place. He's being too forceful, and I gag. I breathe through my nose, trying to stop the spasms that threaten to take over. Now would be the worst possible time to blow chunks. I try to block everything out and focus on my escape route. I need to loosen his grasp so I can get away from him. Placing my hands over his,

I push them down, making him believe I want him to touch me lower. He takes the bait. His grip on my face loosens, and his fingers start to trail down my throat. He allows me to rise a bit in his lap to gain better access. He says a few crude things as his hands travel up the insides of my thighs.

I don't know if I can do this. My heart is beating so hard, slamming against my ribs, and it's all I can do to swallow my screams. I'm standing gingerly on the balls of my feet with my head tipped backward, as Phillip grabs my crotch and gropes my ass through my jeans. He's laughing and he never sees it coming.

I lift up my knee and bring it down right on Phil's crotch. The movement looks innocent at first. It isn't until his ungodly shriek fills the room that they realize what I did. Phil releases me, screaming, and folds in half while I jump off his lap and run. I don't look back. There are yells and feet pounding behind me. Someone is screaming and I'm not sure if it's me. I make it to the door and start to key in the code. The footfalls are closer. The angry words get louder. I gasp for air, as panic strangles me. If this doesn't work…

The keypad makes a high-pitched beeping sound, and a green light blinks. The door is unlocked. I turn the handle and push the door open, shoving into the office.

I'm frozen in place, startled. The office isn't empty. Two men are sitting at Ricky's desk. I let out a sigh of relief when I see Congressman Gambino, Philip's dad, sitting there. He'll help me, he's one of the good guys. Both men look up in surprise. Mr. Gambino stands up quickly. The other man tenses in his seat, instinctively reaching for the inner pocket of his leather jacket.

Bodies press up against my back. Phil and his asshat friends. They've caught up with me, but it's okay. I have Mr. Gambino to help me. He walks up to me and places his hands on my forearms, his eyes scanning over me, questioningly. "Regina? What are you doing here?"

"Mr. Gambino. Your son. His friends. Help me. Please." I'm breathless, unable to string more than two words together at a time, but I need to tell him so he can stop them.

Mr. Gambino looks to the men behind me. "Boys. I'm disappointed in you. You involved Granz's daughter in this? He's a friend of the family. This is sloppy."

Sloppy? Involved? What the hell? I take in my surroundings and notice things I didn't notice when I first stepped in. There are stacks of money on the desk, a small mirror with a fine line of white powder, a plastic bag with even more white powder, and that blonde-haired man, the one sitting with Mr. Gambino. He has an open briefcase in front of him with stacks of money and more clear plastic bags, some filled with powder, some filled with dried leaves.

No. Oh my god. I want to cry. I rushed into a drug deal.

“Ferro needed to learn his place, Dad.” Phil says from behind me. Mr. Gambino pinches the bridge of his nose and sighs, shaking his head as if his son is giving him a headache.

The other man stands up and takes his hand out of his jacket, luckily, not holding anything. I was half expecting him to pull out a gun. The guys behind me are breathing down my neck, and I try to squirm away from them, but there’s no place to go.

“Mr. Gambino, please, let me go. I swear I won’t say anything to anyone. Please.” I hate feeling weak, but I’m caught. There’s no way out now.

Mr. Gambino starts to speak, but the other man talks over him in a raspy voice. “Of course, sweetheart. You!” The man singles out one of Philip’s friends who steps in closer. “Take her home.” The way he says it makes me want to puke. I’m not going home. No one is ever going to see me again.

“Yes, sir,” the young man says walking up behind me, pressing a hand to my back to make me walk.

Zeke starts to whoop and cheer, pointing at Philip.

Before he can speak, the dealer says, “No one is fucking her. She’s going home. Immediately.” He stands up and walks slowly to me. The man is tall. Under his jacket, he wears a deep v-neck tee, emphasizing his muscular frame. His gaze travels up and down my body, assessing me.

His mouth lifts to one side, making the jagged scar on his cheek more obvious. “You say she’s involved with one of the Ferro boys? You guys are fucking idiots. Get her out of here and come back when you're done. And I swear to God, if the cops find any of your DNA on her corpse, I’ll personally break into your jail cell and cut your dick off myself.”

There’s a pause, a breath of silence as I mutter the word. "Corpse? I thought you were taking me home?" My voice is way too high and trembles as I speak.

The man with the scar turns to me, his eyes sweeping over my body. “It’s a damn shame to waste a piece of ass like yours, but business is business. And in this field, home is your final resting place. Get her out of here.”

The world around me spins out of control as the air is sucked from my lungs. My knees buckle. The last thing I see before blackness consumes me is a faint golden glimmer coming from drug guy's mouth as he sneers.

NOT THIS AGAIN!

November 17th, 1:13am

Smoke.

I'm trapped in my nightmare once more. I try to wake up, but I can't. I have to wait for the dream to run its course. The toxic fumes surround me, dancing around like a ghost, an intense heat wafts off of the flames, caressing my bare arms and face. I wait for the image to come into focus, expecting the flames to morph into people that try to pull me down.

The images never come. Awareness slowly settles in, lifting the dream. I feel myself waking up, regaining control of my body once more, but the nightmare goes on. The smell of burning plastic and wood is more prominent as the seconds slowly pass. I try to breathe through my nose, but it burns. I open my mouth to take in a breath, but I can't. There's something over my mouth, keeping it shut. I move my arms to reach up, to take it off, but my hands won't move. They are bound behind my back, making my shoulders burn with every tug. I open my eyes, but my right eyelid won't cooperate. It's heavy and feels thick. My left eye sees perfectly, though, causing me to panic.

I see tall beams of ancient wood reach high into the air. They're sided with old boards, weathered with age. The floor is a mixture of dirt, sawdust, and animal droppings. There are bails of hay stacked opposite me. There's an old green tractor parked next to the door, a fuel container tipped to its side next to it. The flames are stronger in that spot, as if the fuel was used to get the fire started, creating a wall of fire across the door. I can't escape.

Philip. He and his friends did this. They were ordered to get rid of me. 'Corpse,' the blonde man had said. They want me dead and this time, there's no saving me. I'm tied to a chair, my hands behind my back and my ankles bound together. I can't breathe through my mouth because it's been taped closed.

I can feel myself hyperventilating, the tape sucking into my mouth with every breath. I try to push it off with my tongue, but it doesn't work. I thrash my head left and right with no success. I let out a muffled scream, hoping someone, anyone, will hear me. I jump, but my chair catches in the dirt and wobbles, almost toppling me over. If I fall over, there is no way I'll be able to get back up.

There's nothing left to do.

Five months ago, my biggest remorse was that I hadn't claimed my life for my own, that I hadn't done anything worthwhile. I cling to memories I'm proud of--swing dancing, making new friends, living on my own for a brief moment, skydiving, getting a tattoo, riding on the back of a motorcycle, and Peter.

Tears fill my eyes, thinking of him. He's my only regret. I never got to tell him I love him. Right or wrong, he poured his heart out to me, and when he asked me to follow him, I turned away, too crippled by fear to act.

Now, he'll never know he was loved, too.

Flames lick the boards behind me, climbing higher and higher. The heat is becoming unbearable, and it's like trying to breathe tar through my nose. I can't get enough air no matter how hard I try. The flames dance around me, merging into one another, caressing the walls. It's only a matter of time before they reach the rafters above me, and cause the gables to come crashing down. I wonder what will kill me first, the smoke or the roof.

A sudden crash and the sound of breaking glass startles me. It's so hot that any glass in here will explode. The noise comes from behind me. I can't turn around to see what was decimated.

"Gina? Gina, are you in there? Please answer me. Gina?" Peter's voice is coming from a window behind me. I scream through the tape. The resulting sound is weak and muffled. There's no way he can hear me. He'll think I'm not here, and he'll leave.

I hobble on the chair, trying to turn around, but the chair sticks to the floor. I come crashing down, slamming my left shoulder on the ground and hitting my head on the dirt floor. The air is much cooler down here and easier to get into my lungs. Fresher air is coming through the broken window. The breeze is welcoming except that the flames seem to be feeding off the new source of oxygen. They're spreading more rapidly than before.

Facing the window, I manage to see Peter peering inside. When our eyes meet, his face is horror-struck. He wraps his fist with his jacket and knocks out the remaining jagged pieces of glass clinging to the frame. He climbs inside through the opening and drops down to the floor, crouched down close to the ground.

Another voice calls out. "Is she there?" It's Erin. She's outside, just beyond the open window. Pete turns to the window and says, "Yeah, she's here. Stay where you are. I'll get her out."

Peter runs to me and kneels in the dirt, brushing hair away from my face. "What did they do to you? I need to get you out of here. You're safe now." I nod, turning my head to look up at the ceiling with my bad eye. Flames flicker at the corner of my limited line of sight. Peter's forehead beads with sweat, but his hands work fast. They tear at the tape on my ankles. He moves to the back of the chair. "This is going to hurt. I'm so sorry." He rips the tape off of my wrists. I scream into my gag. If I have any skin left on my wrists, it'll be a miracle.

I'm finally free of the chair, and Pete helps me up. The old barn creaks and cracks, making me jump. We both look up and then back at each other. I rip the tape off of my mouth myself and let out a mother of a scream. Pete grabs my arm and pulls me toward the window. It's too high for me to reach it on my own, so he lifts me up and pushes me through.

Erin is on the other side, waiting to help me out. When both my feet are safely on the ground, she takes me into a tight hug, yelling in my ear, "You stupid, idiotic, foolish, dimwitted, lying, irresponsible,--"

"I love you too, Erin."

We wait for Pete to make his way out of the barn. I turn to look through the window. Pete takes a couple of steps back. He's getting ready to run and jump out, but the sound of metal torquing followed by a huge crack shakes the ground as the ceiling falls. Pete vanishes from sight.

Erin and I both scream and run toward the window. Pete's on his back on the ground, unconscious, a broken beam next to him.

IT'S NEVER TOO LATE

November 17th, 1:38 am

NO!

Rapidly, I climb onto the bale of hay under the window, giving me extra leverage. I have one leg in, one leg out when Erin pulls me back. "Gina, don't go in there. You'll die."

I turn toward my friend and practically growl in her face, "So could Peter. I'm going in and you are NOT stopping me. I have to, Erin. I love him."

Erin takes a second and nods. "Right. Okay, then. Let's save your sexy man-beast." She backs up a step and lets me go in. I land on the ground and assess the situation. The fire has continued to spread, and the heat is unbearable. Huge clouds of black smoke billow through the roof and reach into the sky.

I run to Pete's side and put one of his arms around my shoulders. I attempt to lift him up, but he's too heavy.

"You're not THAT strong you dumb twit. Hey, nice tat by the way." I look up. Erin is standing in front of me, hands on her hips, smiling. The ceiling above us creaks and her smile morphs into a frown. She runs to Pete's other side, wrapping his other arm around her shoulders. We drag him toward the window.

"What now, Erin? How are we supposed to get him out there? The window is too high."

"Climb out first, Gee. Once you're outside, reach down for his hands and pull. I'll push him from the bottom. I promise not to grope his ass too much." She smiles crookedly at me.

I'm pulling, and Erin is inside, pushing. Our progress is slow, and I worry a piece of stray glass will dig into his belly, but that's not our biggest problem. He's too big and I'm too weak.

Erin grunts and yells, "Fuck he's heavy! What's he packing, anyway? A whale's dick? And what's in that nutsack of his, horse sperm? Damn! He should go on a diet or something."

My arms are burning. I feel tiny muscle fibers snapping. Pete's hips clear the windowsill, and we finally manage to get Pete out of the building. His limp body rolls off of the bale of hay, onto the ground. I sit next to him, resting his head on my lap and gently stroking the wet hair from his brow. Erin follows shortly after, sitting next to us.

"Thanks." It seems like an understatement, and there's still an inferno at our backs. I look down at Peter and wonder if I'll ever see those sparkling blue eyes again or hear that deep sexy voice.

"No prob." She sucks in fresh air and then coughs up way too much phlegm. "Sexy." She wipes her mouth on the back of her wrist.

I sit at Peter's head, trying not to cry. "He's hurt. He could have died in there."

Erin stands upright again, and when she can speak, she replies, "Yes, he could have, but he didn't. You're not going to lose him. Not tonight. Not because of this. Now, let's drag him farther out. This place could come crashing down at any moment, and we don't want to be anywhere near here when it does. It'll be the world's biggest fireball."

She points to a clearing a couple feet away, and we drag Pete's limp body away from the barn, setting him down gently on his back.

I bend at the waist, my hands propped on my knees, trying to catch my breath. "How did you guys know where to find me?" I'm panting so hard that I start coughing again.

Erin glances at me with a look I've never seen before on her, guilt and shame plastered across her flawless face. "When I came home to find you gone, I figured you'd gone to see Philip at the club, and I panicked. I didn't know what else to do, so I called Ferro. It frightened me to think of what you were potentially walking into. Philip was so angry when you left him. I knew what these guys were into, I just never thought they'd do anything like this."

"They wanted to gang rape me, beat me up and burn me. You knew that?" My shoulders square off as I'm ready to strangle her on the spot.

"Not exactly, but I had an idea of some of it." She won't look at me and wrings her hands behind a spattering of stars. Her face is illumined by dancing flames, defining the slender face I've trusted for years. "I tried to tell you to stay away from him, but you didn't listen. I didn't want to tell you this part."

"Why? Because you thought I wouldn't believe you?"

"No."

"Then you must have thought that I'd be okay. Why else—"

"Gee! Shut up! I knew you wouldn't be okay." Her knuckles are turning white as she strangles her hands. "You don't know all of it."

"Then tell me! Why the hell did my best friend know I was walking into a gang rape and not say anything? Did you think it was funny? Did you—"

Erin is trembling as she screams. "NO! Gina, it was me. I was supposed to be their date for the evening. I was supposed to be there, not you." Tears streak down her cheeks as she speaks.

"Erin?" I step toward her, shocked. I lift my hand to touch her arm, but she jerks away.

Erin doesn't look up. She works her jaw as she wraps her arms around her middle and holds on tight. "I had to cancel with them, because I finally got a meeting with the art gallery. I'm guessing that's when Philip texted you."

"How? Why? Erin, oh my God." I want to cry. Mortification, shame, and fear all collide within me. How could she do this and me not see it? How did I not know?

"Philip and I have been friends forever. When I left my family, it wasn't easy. I struggled a lot, but I didn't want to admit it to you. I didn't want you to think less of me. Some months have been tougher than others. When Philip saw I was struggling, he hooked me up with some people his Dad knew. It was just paid sex with a bunch of his buddies, only a couple of times, and they were never violent."

I want to point out that it's not just paid sex. That it's prostitution, but I don't. I can't hear those words come out of my mouth, so I swallow them back. "Why didn't you tell me?"

Erin points to Peter, who's still unconscious on the ground. "Because you were going to marry this idiot and I thought you were too much of a goody-two-shoes to consider doing anything with another man. It was innocent flirting, and it made you feel so good about yourself. I couldn't take that away from you, not after what Anthony had done to you. Philip really did care for you, and you needed to see that you were worthy of that kind of affection. I swear I didn't know they'd try to hurt anyone. That's not how they work. They just pay to have a good time with consenting girls. When Pete and I got to the club, it was too late, they were stuffing you into the trunk of a car and taking off. We followed them here. There were too many of them, so we hid and waited until they left."

My mouth is hanging open. I shake my head and ask carefully, "That's not what I meant. Why didn't you tell me things were that bad? Why didn't you ask me for help? I could have helped you. This could have been you tonight."

"None of them loved me, so I doubt it. Phil had it really bad for you. That'll drive any man to insanity. And besides, I would have been willing. I'm guessing you put up a bit of a fight to end up banged up like that? You look awful, but I'm proud of you, Gina."

I smile at her comment and look down to Pete. I sit down slowly on the ground next to him and stroke a strand of hair from his forehead with my finger. His chest is rising and falling slowly. My fingers trace the curves of his face, along his jaw and across his lips.

Erin's voice breaks my contemplation. I'd almost forgotten she was here. "You should have seen him tonight. Pete was a total wreck. I think he really cares for you, Gee."

“He told me he loves me."

"Did you say it back?"

"No, and now it’s too late."

Erin wipes the tears off her face, leaving streaks in the soot. Her hair looks like it got stuck in a vacuum cleaner, but she’s still grinning. "It's never too late, babe."

DEER IN THE HEADLIGHTS

November 17th, 2:22am

Erin runs off into the darkness to get the car, leaving me alone with Peter. The light of the burning barn flickers around us, casting eerie shadows on the ground as it echoes the sound of the cracking wood.

I kneel next to him, my trembling hands shaking his shoulders gently. "Wake up, Peter. Please, it's me. Gina. You have to wake up, please!" Shaking his shoulders doesn't work. I slap his cheeks lightly, but Pete's body remains motionless. He looks so peaceful.

It's both beautiful and frightening at the same time. He's usually so full of life, the fighter. He shouldn't be helpless like this. My fingers gently trace the curves of his face. I trace his eyebrows, imagining their usual mocking expression, to his cheeks, where his adorable dimple appears when he smiles, and across to the lips that have kissed me in ways I've never been kissed before.

Fear oozes through my body as I realize he might never wake up. That guy at the rave never woke up. I become frantic, shaking him more vigorously. "Wake up, Pete!"

I can't lose him, not now, not after everything we've been through. My eyes start to burn, and his face blurs in a film of tears.

Trying to blink my tears away, they manage to escape and roll down my cheeks. I comb my fingers through his hair, brushing dark strands away from his forehead. I touch him gently at the place where the beam hit him. My fingers feel something warm and tacky. When I pull my hand away, it's stained red. The hair at the back of his head is sticky with blood and it terrifies me. A sob escapes my lips.

I bend down and place one small, trembling kiss on his mouth, feeling his warmth. He doesn't move. Peter remains still. I don't know what I was expecting. Perhaps I was hoping he'd return the kiss, wrapping his arms around me. He's unconscious. In the real world, kisses don't magically wake people up from whatever is ailing them.

I lower my body down on top of his, my ear resting over his beating heart. I place a hand over his firm chest. His heart is beating strong and fast, and his breathing is slow, deep and steady--all good signs.

I know he can't hear me, but with a shaky voice, I start talking to him anyway. I need to say it before it's too late. Life is fleeting and every second counts. I can't assume there will be time later. Sometimes, later never comes.

"I'm so sorry, Peter. I should have left with you tonight, but I didn't know what to do. It was stupid of me, I know, I just didn't want to believe you. I was afraid you'd hurt me again. I should have listened. I may lose you before I even get a chance to say that--"

I swallow the dry lump in my throat. The words get stuck. Trepidation at being rejected once more is playing tug of war with my words. I can't say it out loud. Every time I've given a piece of myself to Pete, he's returned it, battered and broken. I've had too many regrets over the past few months, and I can't let this be one of them.

"I love you, Peter." Saying it out loud, feels liberating, like I've been held back by heavy chains, pulling tightly around my neck which suddenly vanish. It's bittersweet because all of this is too little, too late. It's opened up a dam, and the words keep coming out and I can't stop them. I just want him to hold me, but his arms lay still along the sides of his body.

My voice is a scratchy mix of sobs and words, sad and happy and desperate. My fingers clutch at his shirt, holding on to him as if my life depends on it. "I love you so much. I have for a long time. I just didn't want to admit it to myself. I believe you, and I want us to try and see if we can be happy together. I want to show you what it feels like to be loved by someone. You deserve to have someone love you and, if you want, I can be that person. Just, please, wake up and stay with me. Don't leave me, Peter. Please, wake up."

I rest my chin on his chest, looking up. I need to see his face. I blink the tears away and blink again. I sniffle back my runny nose. My eyesight is blurry and my eye is swollen, but I see something that gives me hope. His lashes flutter as his eyes move ever so slightly.

I want to call out his name and kiss him, but the faintest ghost of a smile lines his lips, quirking up to one side. A crooked, arrogant, know-it-all smirk blossoms, making his irresistible dimple appear.

A mixture of immense relief, giddy happiness, mortification, and frustrating irritation all fight for first place in this battle of emotions. I can't believe he's smirking! It's that look that makes me want to both kiss him and strangle him all at once.

"Hey Gina."

I blink. "You?" I stutter and shake my head. He was faking? I can't believe he pretended to be unconscious. The ass!

Among my sobs, a laugh manages to escape. He's the most perfect, beautiful, presumptuous, sexy, aggravating ASS! Here I am, pouring my heart out to him and he's just lying here, making me look like a moron while I confess my feelings to him. I hate him, and I love him, and everything is perfect in the world again.

I push myself up and straddle his hips. My hands swat at his chest, hard. "You're such a jerk, Ferro! I take it back, you freaking douche! I take it all back. Every. Single. Word." I'm half-laughing, half-scolding, tears of joy coming down while I slap his chest repeatedly.

Peter starts to laugh and his hands go to my waist. I squeal when he rolls us over, pressing my back to the ground. I'm pinned down by a firm body of toned muscle, caged by two strong arms on either side of me, hypnotized by the most wicked, sexy sneer and the bluest of eyes. I bite down on my lower lip to stop from smiling so big.

"So, I'm a douche, am I?"

"Yes, you are." I try to pout and his eyes soften into a look so tender that I instantly melt inside. He gently wipes a tear away from my right cheek, just under my throbbing eye. The light of the flickering fire beside us is doing wonderful things to his soot-stained face.

"Hey, you." His voice is just as soft as his gaze.

"Hello." I'm suddenly shy, not sure how I should act around him anymore. This is all so new to us, and my head is still a mess, trying to come to grips with everything that has happened in the past twenty-four hours.

Peter dips his head down and drops a small, gentle kiss on my heavy eyelid.

"So, do you still take it back?" Peter lowers himself again and covers my face with light kisses. They travel down my cheek and along my jaw, making it hard to concentrate. He knows what effect he has on me, but his cockiness gives me courage.

"Maybe. It depends. Do you?" I don't even know what I'm saying. Words come out of my mouth on their own.

Pete is nibbling my neck, just under my ear, which makes thinking nearly impossible. He works his way back up to my mouth and, with his lips barely touching mine, says, "I meant every word I said outside the club. I'm not taking any of them back."

With our lips still brushing lightly together, I smile. "Neither do I."

Pete returns the smile and presses his lips onto mine. The kiss deepens and something shifts. Pete lowers his body onto mine, and I wrap my legs around his waist, keeping him close to me. The barn comes crashing to the ground with a thunderous boom, making us jump. The heat is almost too much to bear. Peter looks back down at me. His gaze is as intense as the flames, and it ignites something deep within me.

The emotional rush of the night's events overwhelms me. Adrenaline does weird things to people and I still have a ton of it coursing through my veins. The way he's looking at me makes me hot all over. I spread my hands across his chest, over his shirt and dig my nails in.

Pete's gaze narrows as he looks down on me with devouring eyes. He lets out a sexy sound from deep within, as his lips come crashing down on mine.

The moment is surreal. He's propped on one forearm, his free hand sliding rapidly along my side, past my hip, and back up again. His hand slides up, cupping my breast like he can't touch me fast enough. My hands fly to his hair. He jumps, and I realize I've touched him where he got hit on the head, but that doesn't stop him--or me.

He grinds his hips into mine, and I let out a moan in his mouth, loving the feeling it causes in my core when he pushes down on me. He responds by biting my lower lip and smiling. It's like the kiss in Central Park, but so much more.

My hands travel to his back, and I claw at his shirt, damning it for being there. I want to feel his skin on mine. I reach down and find the hem of the garment before I run my hands up his back, feeling every ridge of every defined muscle under the pads of my fingers. Pete pushes against me once more, rubbing in the right places. He bites down on the sensitive skin of my neck making me gasp. My fingers flex, causing my nails to dig into his skin.

I'm out of control. I've never been this wild before. I'm a ball of lust, but this feels right. Two people who love each other, giving in to each other.

I claw at his back, and his free hand dips lower to unfasten my jeans. His mouth trails searing kisses down my left shoulder, making it sting. I suck in a small hiss through clenched teeth. The pain is excruciating and delicious at the same time. I press my hips up into him, wanting more pressure, more friction, more of everything.

My hands slide down his sides, loving the feel of him beneath my hands. Bright lights flash before us followed by a deafening honk of a horn. I quickly release my grip on Pete and place both hands over my ears. Pete removes his hands from me just as fast and looks down, startled. A car door opens and the sound of footsteps crunching on rough terrain grows louder.

"You two better stop that now. At this point, I don't care which way you swing, Gee, or how long we've known each other--I'll turn this lovey-dovey reunion into a three-way real fast. Christ on a cracker that's hot!" Erin. Always so eloquent.

Pete and I turn our heads toward her, breathing hard, our chests pushing against each other with every breath. All we see is a black silhouette, standing in between us and the glaring headlights.

Pete looks down at me with a glazed look on his face. "She's serious about the three-way thing. You realize that?"

I laugh, a bit stunned at my lascivious behavior. "Oh, believe me, I know." Pete appears stunned by my answer.

"What have you been up to these past couple of weeks?" Pete shakes his head at me in disbelief. He probably thinks that a three-way with Erin is on my been there, done that bucket list of crazy stuff to do, marked finished by a big-ass check.

"Saving myself for you, I suppose?" His eyes study my face for a minute, then fill with remorse. He pushes off of me quickly and extends a hand to help me up. I wrap my arms around his waist, wanting him close, but he removes them gently.

In my ear, he whispers, "I'm so sorry. I shouldn't have taken advantage of you like that just now." He kisses my temple and walks away leaving me completely confused.

I LOVE YOU TOO, ASSHAT!

November 17th, 4:03am

I wake up in the Ferro Mansion to Pete tucking me into my bed. I must have fallen asleep in the car on the ride here. He presses his lips on my forehead, whispering a barely audible, "I love you."

He backs away, heading toward the bedroom door. His words have my skin sizzling, wishing for more. I never dreamed I'd hear him say those words to anyone, least of all to me, but they must be true because he thinks I'm sleeping. There's no reason to lie.

I sit up in bed and call to him. "Wait, Peter?" My voice is thick with sleep and smoke. I feel like I spent the night outside in Erin's neighborhood on garbage day. I'm filthy, I wreak, and I have unidentified crap in my hair. My right eye is throbbing and my tattoo is stinging, but I'm back home safe. Home. For once, the Ferro Mansion feels like a home because Peter is here with me.

He stops in the doorframe and turns around. I can't see his face, it's too dark in the room and the light coming from behind him makes it harder to see his features.

"Stay with me tonight? Please?" I don't want to be alone. I'm tired of being alone. I want to feel safe with him lying next to me.

I can't see him clearly, but I do see his head shake. "I don't think that's such a good idea. I'll see you in the morning." He sounds so tired, physically and emotionally. Apprehension sets in when he mentions morning, like a pin's been pulled from a grenade and at any minute my life could explode.

"Wait!" My voice is loud and slightly panicked. I crawl toward the foot of the bed and Peter meets me half way, sitting on the mattress.

He puts a hand under my chin and his eyes search my face, concerned. "What's wrong?"

"Will I? See you in the morning, that is? I mean are you going to go to the police?" My fingers twist the comforter, mimicking how my insides feel. I don't want him to do it.

Peter's face relaxes. He brushes a thumb across my right eyebrow, and I cringe at his touch. He notices my discomfort and places a small kiss on my eyebrow. When he pulls back, he says, "It goes against my better judgment, but no, I'm not turning myself in—at least not tomorrow. After what almost happened tonight, there is no way I'm ever letting you go again. I don't think I could survive losing you, Gina. I need you."

I climb onto his lap, and take his face in my hands. "I'm here, and I'm safe now. You're not going to lose me." We both lean into a tender kiss. It's not frantic or passionate like outside the barn. This time, it's slow and soft.

His lips sweep over mine like a feather, barely touching me. The kiss is brief. Pete stands up, lifting me with him, my legs around his hips. Pete puts me down gently on the bed and tucks me back in safely under my blankets. He sits next to me with a worried expression on his face.

"Gina, I need to ask you something, and I know this may be hard to answer, but this is important."

Pete exhales and stands up to pace around the room for a few steps. He sits back down, making the bed dip and he rests his elbows on his knees, his head in his hands.

"Peter?" He's starting to scare me. If what he has to ask me has him fidgeting so much, it can't be good.

He lifts his head and closes his eyes as he says, "Did those guys touch you? I mean, I see they weren't very gentle, but did they..." Pete's voice trembles and his hands ball up into fists.

I sit up in bed again and place a hand on his shoulder.

He wants to know if they raped me, but just can't bring himself to say the words. "No. At least, I don't think they did. After they called me a corpse, I wimped out and fainted. I was out of it for the most part, but before I blacked out, their boss, or whoever he was, had specifically said not to touch me. Something about not having their DNA on me."

"Gina, if you don't mind, I'll have a doctor look you over first thing tomorrow morning, just to be on the safe side. I don't trust them to have kept their word and it's taking every ounce of restraint I have not to go find them and..."

Pete's anger is getting the better of him again, it's rolling off of him in waves, so I do the only thing I know how to do to calm him down. I stroke his cheek with my hand. The effect is instantaneous. His shoulders slump and his fists relax. "Hey. It's okay. I don't think they did anything to me other than slap me around and try to kill me a little bit," I grin at him. "But I'll see the doctor tomorrow.

"Get some rest, Gina. I'll see you in the morning." The mattress shifts as Peter gets off of the bed. Before leaving the room, he says, "I love you, Granz."

"You're getting pretty good at saying it, Ferro. You sure you've never done this before?" I tease.

That crooked grin lights up his face. "Smartass."

"I love you too, asshat."

The last thing I hear before falling into a deep, dreamless sleep is Pete chuckling down the hallway.

PETER FERROMONE COLOGNE

November 17th, 9:15am

I step out of my bathroom and into my living room suite, dressed in a fluffy white Ferro robe. As I pad back toward my bedroom, I hear a knock on my door, followed by the sound of footsteps walking away. I open the door and glance down the hallway, but no one is there.

I turn toward Pete's rooms, just across the hall from mine. The door is closed.

Two silver trays are on a serving cart next to my door. I roll it into my suite of rooms and can't help but smile. On one of the trays, there's an impressive selection of breakfast foods. Thick slices of freshly baked bread with fresh butter, a variety of jams and marmalades, crispy slices of bacon, a cup filled with steaming hot coffee with cream and sugar on the side, and a tall glass of fresh orange juice. What makes me smile the most is the single macadamia nut cookie in the center of the platter, right next to a beautiful red rose. There's also a smaller, silver tray with two little white pills, painkillers from the looks of them, ointment for my shoulder, and a cool compress for my eye. He's thought of everything.

As I'm taking my first bite, I notice a note tucked under the plate. The silky smooth vellum paper is cream colored, with the Ferro crest stamped in gold at the top. The scent that drifts under my nose when I pick up the note doesn't go unnoticed, and I laugh, imagining Pete spritzing some of his expensive Venetian Peter Ferromone Cologne on a love letter.

I put my cookie down on the plate - because I totally started with the cookie – grab the rose and read the letter, written with perfect penmanship.

My rose,

I hope you're enjoying your breakfast in bed. The cook thought I was going crazy and almost called on the family shrink to have me medicated, but I assured her I've never felt better in my entire life--all thanks to you.

I've arranged to have a doctor come see you in your room this morning. After she leaves, please take your time and meet me in my study. I'll be waiting for you.

Lovingly yours,
Peter

I can't recall ever really swooning over anyone in my life, other than in front of boy band posters and the occasional movie star when I was younger. But this? Holy! Lovey-dovey Pete makes me swoon over toast! I hug the letter to my chest--enjoying the scent of it--and flop down onto my bed.

I reread the note over and over again as I eat breakfast.

WHERE IT COUNTS

November 17th, 10:45am

After the doctor leaves, I scramble to get ready to see Pete in his study. Clothes are flying left and right in my room, trying to find the perfect outfit. I settle on a cute black swing dress with a dark red floral pattern. It laces up the front, like a corset, with black satin ribbon and has black lace trim around the edge of the swishy circular skirt.

My stomach is in knots as I stand in front of the door to his study. I'm going to count to ten and then walk in. Okay, I take a deep breath and exhale loudly.

"You know, it helps if you use your hand to turn the knob. As far as I know, telekinesis doesn't work." He's standing right behind me. Turn around Gina, turn around Gina, turn arou-

"eeep!"

Peter swings me around in a spin, dips me, and simply says, "Hey." For a poet, he's a man of few words this morning. He smiles, and all traces of my nerves dissolve.

"Hey."

He straightens us up and opens the door to the study, letting me go in first. I pad over to the couch and take a seat. Pete sits next to me and takes one of my hands in his.

"So, how did it go with the doctor?" He holds me tightly tracing my fingers one at a time.

"She says there aren't any signs of, um, forced entry, so to speak." My face flames up. I can feel the heat rising from my chest up to the top of my head. This is a conversation I never thought I'd have, but I'm relieved all the same. I didn't think they were down there, but having someone confirm it makes me feel better.

Pete squeezes my hand and looks into my eyes, prompting me to continue.

"Yeah, so, it looks like everything might be okay after all. I need to have more tests done in a couple of weeks to be officially all in the clear.

Until then, she suggests I take all the necessary precautions, just in case. Speaking of which,"

I remove my hand from Pete's and start to play with the fabric of my skirt. This is going to be hard, but I have to do it.

"Gina? This is me, you can tell me anything." Pete lifts my chin up with a finger.

I stand up and walk over to his desk and pick up the book I saw yesterday. I hand it to him, open to that poem. He takes the book from me and looks at it with curiosity in his eyes.

"Is it story telling time? I don't-"

I sit down next to him and cut him off. "It's about the women, Peter. I'm not okay with them. I know you've had a messed up life with screwed up parents. I know women come and go in this place, but I can't do it. I can't be someone's second best anymore. I'm sorry. If I can't be the only one, I can't be anything at all." My lip trembles as I suck in a breath. We've only just begun, and I'm already giving ultimatums.

Pete sets the book down next to him and takes hold of my hands. He hunches down so that his face is right in front of mine. "Gina, I don't expect you to believe me, but I hope you will. There hasn't been anyone except you for a really long time."

"Twenty-four hours isn't a long time for most people, Peter." I say, not looking up.

He lets go of one of my hands and his thumb strokes my cheekbone. "Silly girl. I haven't been with anyone else since the first night I brought you to my room from the club. After that night, other women are completely unappealing."

I rip my hand out from his grip and stand up, taking a few steps away from the couch. Shaking my head, I put a hand in front of me in a stop motion, in case he has any ideas of coming close and short-circuiting my brain with his touches and kisses.

"Please don't patronize me, Peter. I may be naïve and over-trusting sometimes, but I'm not stupid. There have been plenty of women since that night. I'd rather you be honest with me than have you lie to my face. All those pictures I saw in the news, the stripper across the street from Erin's, those women you left with at the merger gala and that pretty girl wearing a sheet in the ballroom—" My voice cracks at mid-sentence, as my insides twist when I remember that specific girl. She wasn't random.

Pete runs a hand through his hair and leans back into the couch, letting his head fall back on the backrest. "What pretty girl in the ballroom?"

"Really? You don't even remember your last screw from twenty-four hours ago? I'm talking about the girl who interrupted us when we were dancing in the ballroom yesterday. You know, Miss

Bedsheets? You don't bring women home unless--unless they mean something to you." Like I meant something to him that night.

"If you hadn't stormed off yesterday, I could've explained. That damned temper of yours is going to be a problem if you run away from me whenever we have a misunderstanding. That girl was Jon's date, not mine."

"Then why was she looking for you, all naked and smelling like sex while half-dressed with a condom in your back pocket?"

"What? She wasn't looking for me, she was looking for Jon. She probably assumed I was Jon because my back was turned to her. You know my brothers and I look alike."

"And the condom?"

"I can't believe I'm being condemned for being responsible. Gina, I've been putting one of those in my back pocket since the day I discovered sex. It's become a habit, a good habit. Before I leave my rooms, I grab my wallet, my phone, and a condom. Habits are hard to break, half the time I don't even realize I do it. I had no intention of using it."

"You didn't?"

He shakes his head. "No. And the other women were just for show. At first, I was trying to get my mother to see that her plan wasn't working so she could let you off the hook. Nothing happened with any of them, and it's not from lack of trying. I tried, believe me, I tried. I'm not a saint. I was trying so hard to purge you from my mind. I thought maybe, by touching someone else, my hands would forget how soft your skin is, and if I let myself kiss someone else, my mouth would forget the taste and feel of your lips. Whenever the time came, I just couldn't do it. Everything felt wrong, lifeless. I couldn't have sex with any of them."

My throat is so tight that I can't swallow. My face twitches, lost between a smile and a sob. "You couldn't?" He shakes his head. "Why not?"

Peter lowers his lashes and takes a deep breath. When his gaze meets mine, those azure eyes bore into me. "Because they weren't you."

"And the stripper? The girl across from Erin's place? That was just for kicks? That hurt me, a lot." I want to cry and laugh. My body is spazzing between emotions as fear drips down my spine.

"I was purposefully trying to hurt you. I wanted you to hate me so much you'd run far away from me and straight into Gambino's arms."

"What? How could you say that? I mean—"

He cuts me off. "I love you, Gina. I have for a while, but it's killing me. I want you for myself more than I want my next breath, but I also want what's best for you, which is someone better than me. During the merger gala, I saw how good Gambino was for you, how perfect you were for each other, but then I found out about his father. I stumbled across some papers in my mother's office while looking for your criminal file. That's when I discovered the Congressman's involvement with some sketchy people. Why my mother has such information on file is beyond me, but it was there. When Erin called, she confirmed my suspicion that his son was just as corrupt."

Peter sucks in air and runs his fingers through his hair. His head tips to the side and he tries to explain things to me. "I'm not a good man, Gina. The only decent thing I've done was saving you that night at the rave. Even then, you wouldn't have needed saving if it hadn't been for me. You can't marry me, because I don't want your life to be tainted by all the crap I've done—and if you stay with me, that's exactly what will happen. You deserve someone better who'll take care of you better than I ever could." It's as if there's more he wants to say, but the words stop.

After a moment, I gently prod. "But…?"

He glances up at me from under those dark lashes. "But, at the same time, I can't live without you. I need you Gina. You're air, you're light, you're life. I can't walk away, but I can't stay. I'm completely and totally fucked."

I walk back to the couch and sit on Pete's lap, straddling his legs. I take his face in my hands and kiss him. Pete kisses me back, but then pulls away and turns his head to the side, like he doesn't deserve my kiss. He just doesn't see how amazing he is.

"Peter, I want you to listen very carefully. In the past year, there have been three men in my life. Anthony was a hard working scholar on his way to becoming a dedicated doctor. My parents adored him. He ended up cheating on me and pretended to love me to get some fast money. Philip was perfect--a gentleman, well educated, the rich son of a well-known and loved Congressman. But then he tried to rape and kill me. And then there's you—"

He's shaking, and his eyes are looking anywhere but at mine. "Don't. Gina." It's like he's gasping for air, drowning in fear. I can't let him stay there.

"Peter Ferro, the notorious womanizer, violent fighter, and loyal friend who has helped and protected me from the moment we met. On the outside, those two other men were picture perfect, but both ended up hurting me deeply. If what you just told me is true, then you, Peter Ferro, are perfect where it counts the most, right here." I lean in and place a kiss on his chest, over his shirt. Peter holds me there, close to his heart, inhaling sharply. I press my cheek to his chest and feel the comforting beat of his heart.

PRE-ORDER THE FINAL VOLUME of the LIFE BEFORE DAMAGED SERIES

LIFE BEFORE DAMAGED

Volume 10

THE FERRO FAMILY

COMING SOON:

To ensure you don't miss H.M. Ward's next book, text AWESOMEBOOKS (one word) to 22828 and you will get an email reminder on release day.

*****

Want to talk to other fans?

Go to Facebook and join the discussion!

MORE FERRO FAMILY BOOKS

NICK FERRO

~THE WEDDING CONTRACT~

*****

BRYAN FERRO

~THE PROPOSITION~

*****

SEAN FERRO

~THE ARRANGEMENT~

******

PETER FERRO GRANZ

~DAMAGED~

******

JONATHAN FERRO

~STRIPPED~

******

MORE ROMANCE BY H.M. WARD

SCANDALOUS

SCANDALOUS 2

SECRETS

THE SECRET LIFE OF TRYSTAN SCOTT

DEMON KISSED

CHRISTMAS KISSES

SECOND CHANCES

And more.

To see a full book list, please visit:
www.sexyawesomebooks.com/#!/BOOKS

CAN'T WAIT FOR H.M. WARD'S NEXT STEAMY BOOK?

☆☆☆☆☆

Let her know by leaving stars and telling her what you liked about

LIFE BEFORE DAMAGED, VOL. 9

in a review!

COVER REVEAL:

CPSIA information can be obtained
at www.ICGtesting.com
Printed in the USA
LVHW041152070419
613259LV00002B/467